A Hanukkah
with Mazel

For my parents, who I know are smiling down on me –J.E.S.

To Nico, Ariadne and Jason –E.V.

KAR-BEN PUBLISHING
A division of Lerner Publishing Group, Inc.
241 First Avenue North
Minneapolis, MN 55401 USA
1-800-4-KARBEN

Website address: www.karben.com

Main body text set in Avenir LT Std regular.

Library of Congress Cataloging-in-Publication Data

Names: Stein, Joel Edward, author. | Vavouri, Elisa, illustrator.
Title: A Hanukkah with Mazel / by Joel Edward Stein ; illustrated by Elisa Vavouri.
Description: Minneapolis : Kar-Ben Publishing, [2016] | Summary: "Misha has no one to celebrate Hanukkah with until he discovers a hungry cat in his barn. The lucky little cat inspires Misha to turn each night of Hanukkah into something special"— Provided by publisher.
Identifiers: LCCN 2015040985 (print) | LCCN 2016004621 (ebook) | ISBN 9781467781718 (lb : alk. paper) | ISBN 9781467781763 (pb : alk. paper) | ISBN 9781512409369 (eb pdf)
Subjects: | CYAC: Hanukkah—Fiction.
Classification: LCC PZ7.1.S743 Han 2016 (print) | LCC PZ7.1.S743 (ebook) | DDC [E]—dc23

LC record available at http://lccn.loc.gov/2015040985

Manufactured in the United States of America
1 – CG – 7/15/16

A Hanukkah with Mazel

Joel Edward Stein

illustrated by Elisa Vavouri

KAR-BEN
PUBLISHING

Misha was a very good artist but a very poor man. He lived by himself in a tiny cottage outside the village of Grodno. Few people in Grodno had enough money to buy his paintings, so Misha made do with very little. He lived on the few potatoes he grew in his yard and the milk he got from his old cow, Klara.

One winter night when the winds howled and the snow blew around the windows, a little cat wandered into Misha's barn. She made her way to the stall where Klara was sleeping and curled up beside the old cow for warmth. Klara didn't mind having a visitor, and she gave her approval with a low "moo."

In the morning when Misha came to milk Klara, he saw the cat huddled in a corner of the stall, so weak she could hardly walk.

"My, my, what have we here?" Misha said to the cat. "Where did you come from?"

The cat looked up at him with her emerald green eyes. She seemed to sense that Misha was a kind man.

"You're so thin," Misha said in a soothing voice. "Poor old Klara doesn't have much milk to give, but we can share."

Misha took the cat back to his cottage and gave her a dish of milk. She weakly lapped it up, and purred gratefully.

"It's a good thing you wandered in here," Misha said. "I don't think you would have survived the cold night outside."

The cat curled up on a blanket that Misha set down near the fireplace.

"Now, get some rest and you'll feel better soon," said Misha to the cat. "I think I'll call you Mazel. You're certainly a very lucky cat to have wandered out of the cold and into my barn."

In the afternoon, Misha brought Mazel another dish of milk.

"My cupboard is almost empty," said Misha. "But tonight is the first night of Hanukkah and I am making latkes. We will celebrate together."

He went to his pantry, where he found two potatoes and
enough oil to fry the latkes.

"I'll grate the potatoes the way my grandmother taught me,"
Misha said to Mazel. "We'll add a little oil to the pan. A little salt.
A little pepper. And we'll have our Hanukkah latkes."

"And tonight we must light the first Hanukkah candle." On the mantel over the fireplace stood a beautiful silver menorah with figures of two bold lions holding the Ten Commandments.

"My grandfather made this wonderful menorah," Misha said to Mazel. "I have no money for candles, so I don't know how we will light them, but Hanukkah is a time for hope."

Suddenly, Misha had an idea. "I may not have candles," he said to Mazel, "but I am an artist, and an artist has paint!"

Misha took a fresh canvas and stood it on his easel. He dabbed his brush in the paint and made a bold stroke on the canvas. As Mazel watched, Misha painted a beautiful large menorah just like the one that stood on the mantel. Then he painted all the candles, including the shammash.

"Now we're ready for Hanukkah!"

At sundown, when it was time to light the first Hanukkah candle, Misha sang the blessing as he painted one flame on the shammash and another flame on the first candle.

Then he sat down to eat his latkes. He put one latke into Mazel's dish. Mazel gave a "meow" of approval and licked her whiskers.

The next night, when Misha went to the easel to draw the next candle flame, he saw how little paint he had left. "We will have to make these paints last as long as we can, Mazel," he said.

By the fourth night of Hanukkah, Misha had run out of yellow paint. So he made do with a little blue, a little orange, and a little red.

On the eighth night, Misha sang the blessing and used the last drops of paint to make the final flame.

The next afternoon, there was a knock at the door. Through the window Misha could see the horse and wagon of a peddler. He opened the door to greet a small man with a big smile.

"Shalom, shalom," the man said cheerfully. "I'm Meyer the merchant, and I sell many things. Perhaps I have something you would like to buy?"

"I'd love to see what you have," said Misha, "but I have no money to buy your goods."

"Well, perhaps you have something you can trade then," suggested Meyer, peeking around the door.

Misha smiled. "I am an artist, and an artist has paintings!"

He led Meyer inside and showed him his paintings. Meyer looked at scenes from Misha's childhood and paintings of Jewish holidays and weddings. A portrait of a little cat caught his eye.

"These are wonderful," said Meyer.

They heard a loud "meow" as the cat scampered toward them, purring loudly.

"Goldie? Is it really you?" exclaimed Meyer, scooping Mazel into his arms.

"Goldie?" Misha looked from Mazel to Meyer.

"Yes! I have had her since she was a tiny kitten," said Meyer. "A few nights ago, while I was asleep, she must have jumped out of the wagon. I've been looking for her."

"So that means . . . Mazel is Goldie!" cried Misha.

Meyer looked confused. "Mazel?"

"I found her in my barn one morning," Misha explained.
"She was very weak. So I took her in and cared for her. She
was lucky to find my barn and I was lucky to find her."

"Yes, now I see why you named her Mazel," said Meyer. "She certainly was lucky."

Misha tried to smile. Mazel had become his good friend. But now he realized that she would have to go back to her owner.

Meyer turned to the paintings.

"You have quite a collection here," he said. "I especially like that wonderful menorah painting on the easel. I know many people who would be interested in buying paintings like these. Would you be interested in selling them to me?"

"Of course!" said Misha. He helped Meyer load the paintings into the wagon.

"You know," Meyer said, "I'm on the road a lot, and I wonder if you would do me a small favor. Could you take care of Goldie—I mean Mazel—for me?"

A broad smile appeared on Misha's face. "That is not a favor," he said. "That is a gift."

Mazel weaved back and forth between Misha's and Meyer's legs, purring happily.

Meyer climbed up on his wagon. He waved to
Misha and Mazel as he drove slowly away.
"I'll be back!" he shouted. "Happy Hanukkah
to both of you!"